# The Toy House Dolls

Original title: Open the Door and See All the People

# The Toy House Dolls

by CLYDE ROBERT BULLA

Pictures by WENDY WATSON

SCHOLASTIC INC.
New York  Toronto  London  Auckland  Sydney  Tokyo

ISBN 0-590-09835-7

Text copyright © 1972 by Clyde Robert Bulla. Illustrations copyright © 1972 by Wendy Watson. This edition is published by Scholastic Inc., by arrangement with Thomas Y. Crowell Company, publishers of the book under the title OPEN THE DOOR AND SEE ALL THE PEOPLE.

12 11 10 9 8 7 6 5 4                                    5 6 7 8 9/8 0/9

Printed in the U.S.A.                                                    11

# *By The Author*

# CHAPTER ONE

# The Fire

They never knew what started the fire. "A spark from the kitchen stove, maybe," said Mamma. "A little mouse in the box of matches," said Teeney. But they never could be sure.

Jo Ann woke up first. The bedroom was hot and smoky. She woke Mamma, and Mamma got Teeney out of bed.

They climbed out the window. The roof was on fire from one end to the other. They stood in the wet grass and watched the house burn.

Jim and Martha Toller lived on the hill a mile away. Jim was up late, giving medicine to a sick cow. He saw the fire, and he and Martha came down in their car.

"Didn't you save anything?" asked Martha.

"I've got my girls," said Mamma, and she hugged them both.

They went home with the Tollers. In the morning Mamma put on one of Martha's dresses. The girls stayed in bed, because they had nothing to wear except their nightgowns. But soon the neighbors heard what had happened and brought them dresses.

People kept coming to the Tollers' house and talking about the fire.

"I don't want to hear about it any more," said Jo Ann.

"Go out back if you want to," said Mamma. "As soon as I can get away, I'll come out, too."

Jo Ann led Teeney into the orchard. They sat under an apple tree.

Jo Ann was almost eight. Teeney was six. People said they didn't look like sisters at all. Jo Ann's face was thin. She had brown eyes and long, brown hair. Teeney's face was round. Her eyes were green as gooseberries. Her hair was the color of straw, and it wouldn't grow long.

Jo Ann picked up a tiny apple that had fallen off the tree. "Let's play catch," she said, but she could see that her sister didn't want to.

"When are we going back to our house?" asked Teeney.

"Why do you want to go back?" asked Jo Ann.

"Well, I thought I might find Baby," said Teeney.

"You won't find Baby," said Jo Ann. "Everything is gone."

Teeney began to cry.

"My doll is gone, too, but you don't see me crying," said Jo Ann. "You'd better stop it."

But Teeney couldn't stop.

"If you're going to be a baby," said Jo Ann, "get down where nobody can see you!"

While Teeney hid in the tall grass, Jo Ann cried a little, too, but she didn't let her sister see her.

"Listen," she said. "Don't you ever cry in front of Mamma. And don't you ever say a word about your doll or anything else you lost. Mamma already has enough on her mind."

Teeney came up out of the grass. She dried her eyes on the sleeve that came down over her hand. The dress was too big for her. "Crazy old dress!" she said.

"You're lucky to have it," said Jo Ann. "Straighten up now."

Teeney straightened up. Jo Ann threw the green apple, and Teeney caught it. They were playing catch when Mamma came out.

She sat down with them.

"I've been trying to think," she said. "It's hard to think when everyone is talking."

"They all talk at once," said Jo Ann.

"The neighbors have been good to us. Jim and

4

Martha have been the best of all," said Mamma. "But we can't stay here forever, can we?"

Jo Ann shook her head.

"When your father died, I thought about going away," said Mamma, "but you were both so little, and our rent was paid up for a year. I thought it was easier just to stay on the farm. It's different now. Maybe *this* is the time."

"Time for what?" asked Jo Ann.

"Remember the old rhyme?" asked Mamma. "About the church and the steeple?"

Jo Ann and Teeney said it together:

"This is the church,
Here's the steeple.
Open the door
And see all the people!"

"This morning I was thinking," said Mamma. "Maybe now is the time for us to 'open the door and see all the people.'"

The girls looked at each other.

"Maybe it's time we went out into the world," said Mamma. "That's what I mean."

"You mean—go away from here?" asked Jo Ann.

"We've never been anywhere else," said Mamma. "This might be the time to go out and see how other people live."

The girls waited.
"We might go to the city," said Mamma.
They sat and thought about it for a while.

6

Teeney said, "We don't know anybody there."

"I know Lulu," said Mamma.

Lulu was her school friend. They had been girls together. Then Lulu had married and gone away. Mamma had never seen her again, but they wrote to each other.

"I don't want to live with Lulu," said Teeney.

"We wouldn't live with her," said Mamma.

Jo Ann was looking at Mamma's face. "Do *you* want to go to the city?"

Mamma laughed a little. "When I was a girl I was always wanting to go. I wanted to see the lights and the high buildings. I wanted to see the pretty parks with fountains—"

"There's a fountain at school," said Jo Ann.

"That's a drinking fountain," said Mamma. "This is another kind, with water coming out all the time and going high in the air. Wouldn't you like to see one like that?"

Both the girls were quiet.

Mamma said, "If you don't want to go, we'll think of something else. But right now I don't know what else to do."

"Oh, I want to go," said Jo Ann.

"You do? You really do?" asked Mamma.

"Yes," said Jo Ann.

"Then I'll write to Lulu," said Mamma. "I'll write tonight."

# CHAPTER TWO

# Decker Street

Lulu answered Mamma's letter and told them to come. She knew where Mamma could get work. She thought she could even find them a house to rent.

"How will we get there?" asked Jo Ann.

"On the bus," said Mamma.

"Won't that cost a lot?" asked Jo Ann.

"We'll have enough," said Mamma.

They sold the hay in the barn. They sold the cow and calf. With the money they got, Mamma bought the girls each a pair of shoes and a change of clothes. Then she bought the bus tickets to the city. After that, Jo Ann knew there couldn't be much money left.

Jim and Martha took them to the bus. Martha gave them a sack of fried chicken to eat on the way.

Mamma and Teeney sat together. Jo Ann sat just across the aisle. They waved good-bye to Jim and Martha. The big bus began to move, and in half a minute they were out of town.

They saw the country go by. It was fun at first. But the ride went on for a day and a night and part of another day. By that time they were tired.

Mamma said, "Look, girls, here's the city!"

"I see it," said Jo Ann, and Teeney was too tired to say anything.

Lulu met them at the station. She was a big woman, and heavy on her feet. She didn't talk much, but she seemed glad to see them.

She took them home with her in her car. It was an old car with most of the paint off.

She lived in an apartment. Her husband was away, but their daughter was at home. Her name was Nyda, and she was seventeen. She was almost as heavy on her feet as Lulu. The apartment was small. With so many people there, it was crowded.

Lulu made the girls a bed on the sofa.

"It's got lumps," said Teeney.

"Sh! Don't let them hear you," whispered Jo Ann. "We can stand it tonight, and maybe we'll have our own place tomorrow."

In the morning Lulu drove them across the city. She said, "I found this house that you might like. It's on Decker Street."

Teeney looked for fountains, but she didn't see any. She thought there were too many cars, and she was scared when the big trucks came close.

They drove up Decker Street.

"Look—yellow houses," said Jo Ann.

There were blue and green ones, too. There was one the color of strawberry ice cream. The houses were small. Most of them looked old.

Girls and boys were playing on the sidewalks. Some boys were having a ball game in the middle of the street. They didn't want to stop, and Lulu had to honk them out of the way.

She parked the car at the end of the street. "Here's the place."

The house was small and brown. There was a thin tree in front of it. There was a yard with no grass at all.

Lulu had a key. She opened the door and they went in.

"Look at the things here already," said Mamma. "A chair and a sink and an icebox—"

"It's a refrigerator," said Lulu.

Jo Ann had found the bathroom. "Come and look, Teeney. It's pink."

"Is this going to be all right?" asked Lulu. "Of

course, the house is small, and we'll have to clean it up—"

"It's just fine," said Mamma.

"I can let you have some bedclothes," said Lulu, "if you don't mind sleeping on the floor."

"We don't mind, do we, girls?" said Mamma. She told them, after Lulu had gone, "Maybe the place doesn't look like much now, but we can fix it up."

She opened all the windows. She found an old broom and swept the floor.

There were bottles and tin cans in the backyard. The girls picked them all up and put them into a box.

Lulu came back with blankets, sheets, and pillows. She brought some bread and milk and breakfast food.

"I'll be back tomorrow," she said, and she went away.

They had bread and milk for supper. They sat on the front step and watched the lights come on.

"I hear a sound," said Teeney. "It never stops."

"It's the cars on the freeway," said Jo Ann. "You can see it over there."

"Isn't it nice to live where we can see it?" said Mamma.

And they sat there until bedtime, watching the lights on the freeway.

# CHAPTER THREE

# Brenda

Before the end of the week Mamma found work. Lulu helped her.

"It's in a hotel," said Mamma. "All I have to do is make beds and clean the rooms."

"Is it far away?" asked Teeney.

"It isn't close," said Mamma, "but I can get a bus here at the corner. It will take me straight to the hotel. I go at seven and come home at four."

"Every day?" asked Teeney.

"No. I have two days off every week," said Mamma.

"I can take care of things while you're gone," said Jo Ann.

"You won't have to," Mamma told her. "Nyda will come and stay."

Jo Ann frowned. "We don't need her."

"I'll feel better if there's somebody with you," said Mamma. "When fall comes, you girls will be in school. Then we won't need anybody to stay."

On Mamma's first day at work, Nyda came over. She didn't talk much. She just sat on the back step and read magazines.

Jo Ann and Teeney played in the backyard. They played school. Jo Ann was the teacher, and she had found a wooden box for her desk.

"Everybody sit up straight," she said.

"I don't want to play school," said Teeney. "Let's go up the street."

"We have to stay where Nyda can watch us," said Jo Ann.

"Aren't we ever going up the street?" asked Teeney.

"Yes, but not today." Jo Ann went back to playing school. "Sit up straight."

A little dog came running across the yard. He was white, with black ears and a black ring around one eye. He jumped up on the box in front of Jo Ann.

"Teacher, there's a dog on your desk," said Teeney.

"Get down!" said Jo Ann.

A girl was looking through a hole in the fence. "Here, Skipper!" she called. "You come home."

The dog jumped off the box and ran away.

The girl stayed there. "Are you going to live here?" she asked.

"Yes," said Jo Ann.

"You don't have a dog, do you?" asked the girl.

"Not yet," said Jo Ann.

"You can play with Skipper if you want to. He likes everybody," said the girl. "I know your names. You're Jo Ann, and your sister is Teeney."

"How did you know that?" asked Jo Ann.

"I heard you talking. My name is Brenda, and this is Susie." The girl held up a doll for them to see.

"Oh!" said Teeney.

The doll had round, red cheeks and brown eyes and long, dark curls.

"Susie is my new doll," said Brenda. "I got her yesterday."

Teeney said, "I'm going in."

She ran into the house.

"What's the matter with *her?*" asked Brenda.

"I'd better go see." Jo Ann went into the house. She found Teeney in the bedroom, sitting on the floor.

"What did you run away for?" asked Jo Ann.

"That old Brender!" said Teeney.

"*Brenda.* I thought she was nice," said Jo Ann.

"The way she was showing off, just because she's got a doll and we haven't!"

"She wasn't showing off," said Jo Ann. "I think she'd let you play with her doll if you asked her."

"I wouldn't play with her doll," said Teeney. "If I can't have my own—"

"Now don't start that," said Jo Ann. "Come on. Let's go make a playhouse."

"I'm not going out there where *she* is," said Teeney.

"You're being silly. Come on." Jo Ann tried to pick Teeney up off the floor.

But Teeney wouldn't go. She stayed in the house all the rest of the day.

CHAPTER FOUR

# A Surprise

After Mamma had gone to work in the morning, Nyda came again.

"Why don't you girls play outdoors?" she said.

"I don't want to," said Teeney.

"You were in the house all day yesterday," said Nyda. "What's the matter with you?"

"She'll be all right," said Jo Ann, but she worried. Teeney hadn't been hungry at breakfast.

It was a long day. Jo Ann walked around the house a few times. Once she went out into the street and watched some boys kicking a football. She saw Brenda playing with two other girls.

She kept calling, "Teeney, come look," or, "Come show me where you want the playhouse."

But Teeney stayed inside all day.

Mamma was late getting home. As soon as she got there, Nyda left.

Mamma looked happy. "There's a surprise coming."

"What is it?" asked Teeney.

"It wouldn't be a surprise if I told you," said Mamma.

"When is it coming?" asked Jo Ann.

"Maybe this evening," Mamma told her.

"I know what it is," said Teeney.

"You hush!" whispered Jo Ann.

"I know—I know!" Teeney began to dance.

"We'll see if you do." Mamma went into the bedroom to lie down. "Just a minute to rest my back," she said.

Jo Ann asked Teeney, "What do you think the surprise is?"

"Dolls," said Teeney.

"I don't think so," said Jo Ann.

"What else could it be?" asked Teeney.

"It could be a lot of things," said Jo Ann.

Mamma got up, and they had supper. They heard a car stop out in front.

"Maybe that's the surprise," said Mamma.

They all ran to the door. A small truck was parked outside. In the back were a bed and four chairs.

A man got out of the truck. He brought the bed and chairs into the house.

"Thank you, Ben," said Mamma.

"That's all right," said the man, and he drove away.

Mamma told the girls, "I saw these things at the hotel. They were going to throw them away, so I said I'd take them."

"Is *this* the surprise?" asked Teeney.

"Yes," said Mamma. "Isn't it a nice one? And wasn't Ben nice to bring them? He works at the hotel, too."

"We needed a bed and some chairs," said Jo Ann.

"They're old," said Mamma, "but we can paint them, and they'll be as good as new."

"They're pretty, even if they are old," said Jo Ann. "Aren't they pretty, Teeney?"

Teeney didn't answer. She was almost crying, but Mamma didn't see because she was busy putting sheets on the bed.

"This is better than the floor, isn't it, girls?" she said, when they were in bed and the lights were out. "We'll really have a good rest, won't we?"

In the middle of the night Jo Ann woke up. Someone was saying over and over, "I want my doll — I want my doll!"

Mamma turned on the light. Teeney was sitting up in bed. Her eyes were shut. "I want my doll!" she said.

"Teeney —," said Mamma.

Teeney's eyes opened. "Mamma!" she said.

Mamma held her for a while. She said, "You were talking in your sleep."

"Was I?" said Teeney.

She looked at Jo Ann. "I couldn't help it. I couldn't help it if I talked in my sleep."

"Of course, you couldn't," said Mamma. "You

*don't* have a doll, do you? You don't have dolls, either of you."

"We don't need them," said Jo Ann.

"There's been so much to think about," said Mamma. "I just didn't think about dolls."

"We need other things more," said Jo Ann.

"I don't know," said Mamma. "Sometimes you need a doll as much as anything else. I know, because I—" She stopped.

"Because you what?" asked Jo Ann.

"I was remembering when I was little," said Mamma. "I used to go to my grandma's, and she had a doll. It was one she'd had when she was a girl. It was a china doll with the blackest hair and the bluest eyes! She had a red satin dress on it, and I thought it was the most wonderful thing. I wanted that doll—there was nothing else in the world I wanted as much."

"Did you ever get it?" asked Jo Ann.

Mamma shook her head. "I never even got to hold it. It was always up in the cupboard. Well," she said, "we'll find you some dolls. We'll go out together and look. Now are you girls ready to settle down?"

They said they were. Mamma put out the light. And when Jo Ann thought the others were asleep, Teeney said in a sleepy voice, "Mamma, I wish you'd got that doll."

CHAPTER FIVE
# *The Toy House*

In the morning Nyda came again. "I want you both to go out and play," she said. "It's not good for you to stay shut up in the house all the time."

Jo Ann went out. This time Teeney went with her.

"I couldn't help what I said last night," Teeney said. "I was asleep, so I couldn't help it."

"I know you couldn't," said Jo Ann, "but it's too bad you had to talk about dolls. Now Mamma will think she has to get us some."

Brenda's dog came into the yard. He barked, but his tail was wagging.

"There's old Brenda looking through the fence." Teeney made a face. "Let's not look at her."

"She never hurt us." Jo Ann went over to the fence and said, "Hello."

Brenda held up her doll. "I gave Susie a new hairdo."

Teeney went to the fence, too. "We're going to have dolls," she said.

"Are you?" said Brenda.

"Yes, we are," said Teeney.

"They have some nice ones at The Toy House," said Brenda.

"Is that where you got Susie?" asked Jo Ann.

"That's where I get all my dolls," answered Brenda.

"Did she cost a lot?" asked Jo Ann.

Brenda looked surprised. "She didn't cost anything."

"Then how — ?" began Jo Ann.

"I just went and picked her out. You don't pay anything at The Toy House."

Jo Ann said slowly, "You — don't — pay?"

"Oh, no. You borrow what you want, and you can keep it two weeks."

"*Borrow* it?" said Jo Ann.

"You know, like a library book," said Brenda. "Only at The Toy House you get toys instead of books."

"I don't believe it," said Teeney.

"You hush!" Jo Ann asked Brenda, "Who can borrow dolls from The Toy House?"

"Just about anybody," answered Brenda. "They

have things besides dolls. They have scooters and wagons and games—"

"Could *we* borrow things?" asked Jo Ann.

"If your mother signed a card for you," said Brenda, "and you promised to take good care of the things. If you don't take care of them, you can't borrow any more."

"Where is The Toy House?" asked Jo Ann.

"On this street, a long way up. I'll ask my mother if I can show you." Brenda went away.

They waited, but she didn't come back.

"I guess her mother said No," said Jo Ann.

"Do you believe there *is* a Toy House?" asked Teeney.

"She wouldn't make it up, would she?" said Jo Ann.

They could hardly wait for Mamma to come home. When they saw her coming down the street, they ran to meet her. They told her what Brenda had said.

"I never heard of such a thing!" said Mamma.

"I don't see how it could be," said Jo Ann.

"Neither do I," said Mamma, "yet we've got to remember something. We're in the city now, and things are different. Brenda wouldn't make it all up, would she?"

"That's what I said," said Jo Ann.

"It won't be hard to find out," Mamma said.

"We can go see."

"Now?" asked Teeney.

"It's getting late, and we haven't had supper,"
said Mamma, "but tomorrow I have the day off.
Let's wait until then."

# CHAPTER SIX

# Mrs. Lacey

As soon as they had breakfast, they started out. Mamma wanted the girls to find Brenda and ask her again about The Toy House.

But the shades were down at the house next door. "I don't think she's up," said Jo Ann. "We don't need to ask, anyway. She said it was on this street. All we have to do is go until we find it—if it's there."

They walked up Decker Street. They talked about the things they saw.

"That church isn't so big," said Teeney. "Our church at home was bigger."

"Look, a grocery store," said Jo Ann.

"I'm glad we know where it is," said Mamma.

"I can get our groceries there instead of downtown. It's hard to carry them home on the bus."

They saw a brick schoolhouse with swings in the yard.

"Maybe this is where we'll go to school," said Jo Ann.

They went farther and farther up Decker Street. Teeney was walking behind.

"Are you tired?" asked Mamma.

"No," said Teeney.

"We've had a good walk, and we've seen a lot of things," Mamma said. "Maybe we should start back now."

"I'm not tired," said Jo Ann.

They went on to the next block.

"Girls, look at this house," said Mamma. "Isn't it beautiful?"

It was a tall white house behind a row of silver willow trees. One of the trees made a shady place on the sidewalk.

They stopped in the shade. "Let's rest here a minute," said Mamma, "before we go back."

"Mamma!" said Jo Ann. She was looking at the sign on the house. Then Mamma and Teeney were looking at it.

Teeney pulled at Jo Ann's dress. "What does it say—what does it say?"

Jo Ann told her. "It says 'The Toy House.'"

They stood close together outside the iron gate. They hung back, as if they all felt shy.

It was Teeney who pushed the gate open. They went slowly up the walk and onto the porch.

A voice said, "Come in."

Teeney opened the door. They all went inside. They saw a woman sitting at a desk. She smiled at them. She was pretty when she smiled.

"Welcome to The Toy House. I'm Mrs. Lacey," she said. "Aren't you new here?"

"Yes, we are," said Mamma.

"Would you like to take out toys?" asked Mrs. Lacey.

"You really have toys for girls and boys to take out?" asked Mamma. "It doesn't seem real. We just came from the country, and we never heard of anything like this before."

"It was my mother's idea. She started The Toy House years ago," said Mrs. Lacey. "She always wanted to do something for boys and girls, and she thought of this. People came to help us. Now we have twenty people working here."

"Where do you get the toys?" asked Mamma.

"Sometimes people give us their old ones," said Mrs. Lacey. "Sometimes we go out and look for them. If the toys are worn or broken, we try to make them as good as new. Let me show you where we work."

She led them into a room that smelled of paint and glue. Men and women were working at tables. They were mending and painting toys, and they talked as they worked.

Mrs. Lacey led the way into a green room. On tables and shelves were wagons and scooters and little cars and airplanes.

"This is one of our toy rooms," she said.

"All the toys look new," said Jo Ann.

"They do, don't they?" Mrs. Lacey took them into a yellow room. "Here are the games and puzzles."

They went on into a pink room. Mrs. Lacey said, "Here we have the—"

"*Dolls!*" said Teeney, almost in a whisper.

The girls gazed at the roomful of dolls. Dolls on shelves. Dolls on tables. Dolls in boxes. Every kind of doll.

"Look at this one!" said Jo Ann. "Look here, Teeney!"

"Is it dolls you want?" asked Mrs. Lacey. "Would you each like to choose one?"

"*Any* one?" asked Teeney.

"Any one you see," said Mrs. Lacey.

"I wouldn't know how to choose!" said Jo Ann.

"Take all the time you need. When you've chosen, bring the dolls to the desk." Mrs. Lacey left them.

"Girls, come here." Mamma was looking at a doll on a shelf. It had a china head with black hair, blue eyes, and shiny pink cheeks. It had on a long, blue dress with puffed sleeves. "Do you remember the doll I told you about? The one my grandma had? It looked like this, only hers had a red dress."

"It's pretty," said Jo Ann. "It's an old-fashioned doll."

Teeney was holding a baby doll with a yellow curl on top of its head. "I want this one."

"Are you sure?" asked Jo Ann

"I'm sure," said Teeney.

It took Jo Ann longer to choose. The doll she chose had real hair and eyes that opened and shut.

Mamma was still looking at the old-fashioned doll. She touched it. Then she and the girls went back to the desk.

Mrs. Lacey gave each of the girls a Toy House card, and Mamma had to sign both cards.

"Now you may borrow the dolls for two weeks," said Mrs. Lacey. "You'll take good care of them, won't you?"

"Oh, yes," said Jo Ann.

"Yes, they will," said Mamma.

They thanked Mrs. Lacey and started home.

"Look at us," said Teeney. "We're a big family now!"

41

# CHAPTER SEVEN

# The Dolls

Jo Ann wondered if their dolls had names.

"Do you think we should go back to The Toy House and find out?" she asked.

"I've already named mine," said Teeney. "Her name is Baby."

"I want to call mine Kathy," said Jo Ann, "if you think Mrs. Lacey won't care."

"She won't care," said Mamma.

With dolls in the family, everything was different.

"There's more to *do*," said Teeney.

Brenda came to see their dolls. Two other girls, Maggie and Anita, came, too, and they all played picnic.

After that, Jo Ann and Teeney took their dolls over to Maggie's. Nyda said it was all right as long as they didn't go far.

They were playing at Brenda's one afternoon. Teeney liked Brenda now and was glad she lived next door. Brenda had a set of doll dishes, and they were having a tea party behind the rosebush.

Brenda's dog came to the party. He ran across the tablecloth and left paw-prints. He tipped the dolls over.

"He keeps trying to lick Baby's face." Teeney scolded Skipper. "You better stop that!"

Brenda caught Skipper and tied him up in the garage. She dusted off her doll. "I'll have to wash Susie's dress before I take her back to The Toy House. I'm getting a new doll next Tuesday."

"Doesn't it make you feel bad to give up Susie?" asked Jo Ann.

"Not as long as I can have another doll," said Brenda.

"I'd rather keep the one I have," said Jo Ann.

"So would I," said Teeney.

"Do we have to give up these dolls?" asked Jo Ann. "Can't we just go on borrowing the same ones?"

"You can if you want to. You can even adopt them," said Brenda. "I'm not sure how you do it, but you can find out."

"What is 'adopt'?" asked Teeney.

Brenda told her, "It's when you keep a doll and she's yours forever."

"That's what I want," said Teeney.

It was what Jo Ann wanted, too. The girls talked to Mamma about it when she came home.

"Brenda says there's a way to adopt our dolls," said Jo Ann.

Teeney had hold of Mamma's hand. "Let's go to The Toy House and find out how."

"Not now," said Jo Ann. "Mamma's tired."

"I'm not so tired," said Mamma. "We can go now, if you don't mind waiting for supper."

They went to The Toy House. Mrs. Lacey was at the desk.

"My girls want to adopt their dolls," said Mamma. "They heard there's a way."

"There is a way." Mrs. Lacey told them the rules. "Every two weeks you bring your dolls in. We look at them to see that they are getting good care. We want to be sure they have a good home."

"We give them a good home," said Teeney.

"After six weeks," said Mrs. Lacey, "if you've taken good care of your dolls, you'll get your certificates."

"What are they?" asked Jo Ann.

"A certificate is a paper that shows the doll is yours." Mrs. Lacey looked at the cards on her desk. "You have one week to go on your first two weeks. Bring your dolls back in a week. After that you bring them twice more—"

"Once every two weeks," said Jo Ann.

"That's right," said Mrs. Lacey.

Jo Ann said on the way home, "Only five more weeks, and we can adopt our dolls."

And that night they heard Teeney saying to Baby, "In five weeks I'm going to adopt you, and you'll be mine forever."

# CHAPTER EIGHT

# Saturday Morning

A week went by. It was time for the girls to take their dolls to The Toy House. They waited until Mamma came from work, and she went with them.

Mrs. Lacey was out. A man from the workroom was at the desk. His name was Mr. Dahlman, but everyone called him The Doll Man because he mended dolls. His hair was white, and he had stooped shoulders, but his face looked young, almost like a boy's.

"My girls are adopting their dolls," Mamma told him. "Will you look and see if they're taking good care of them?"

The Doll Man set the dolls on the desk. He looked at their hands and faces and clothes. "Oh, yes, they look very neat," he said. "Very neat, indeed. You know the rules, don't you? Bring them back in two more weeks."

The next two weeks passed, and the girls took their dolls to The Toy House again. This time Mrs. Lacey was there. She smiled when she looked at the dolls. "I can see you're giving them a good home," she said.

That left only two weeks.

Time went slowly for Jo Ann and Teeney. For Mamma it went faster. "I wanted to make you dresses to wear when you go to adopt your dolls," she said, "but there won't be time enough."

"We don't need new dresses," said Jo Ann.

"Anyway, your dolls can have something new," said Mamma.

Lulu had given them some scraps of cloth. Mamma spread them out on the bed. "What about the stripes for your doll, Jo Ann? Teeney, would you like this blue for Baby?"

She began to cut and sew. Almost before the girls knew it, the dresses were finished. Jo Ann and Teeney dressed the dolls in their new clothes and walked them across the bed.

"It's a parade," said Teeney.

"A fashion parade," said Jo Ann.

Mamma looked at the scraps that were left. "There's enough for a doll blanket. Who wants a doll blanket?"

"Make it for Teeney," said Jo Ann, "because her doll is a baby."

The next night Mamma made a blanket for Teeney's doll.

Teeney said, "Wait till they see Baby with her new dress and blanket. Then they'll *know* this is a good home."

The day came—the last day of the last two weeks. The girls dressed their dolls. Teeney wrapped Baby in her new blanket.

Mamma came home, and they all went to The Toy House.

Mrs. Lacey was at the desk. "Have the last two weeks gone already?" She looked into the box of cards. "Yes, they have. And you've taken good care of your dolls, I can see that. Did you make the new clothes for them?"

"Mamma made them," said Teeney.

"I'm sure your dolls have a good home," said Mrs. Lacey. "Could you come to the adoption party on Sunday? Sunday afternoon at two?"

"Could we, Mamma?" asked Jo Ann.

"Your adoption certificates will be ready. Some other girls will be adopting their dolls, too," said Mrs. Lacey. "The party will be in the playroom. You know where it is? Just next to the doll room." She said to Mamma, "Of course, we want you to come, too."

Mamma looked pleased and surprised, and her face turned pink. "Oh, thank you. I will if I can."

They talked all the way home.

"We really get to adopt our dolls!" said Teeney.

"We're going to get certificates," said Jo Ann.

Mamma said, "There's going to be a party."

That was Friday. On Saturday morning Brenda came by. "Come and see the race!" she shouted through the door.

Jo Ann was in the house, talking with Nyda.

"What race?" she asked. "Who's racing?"

"Max and Lennie—they've got new wagons, and they're going to race them. You better hurry. They're about to start." Brenda ran on up the street.

Teeney was in the backyard. Jo Ann called out to her, "There's going to be a race. Come on if you want to see it," and she ran after Brenda.

Max and Lennie were two boys from the next block. They had their wagons on the sidewalk, and they were going to race downhill. Boys and girls had come to watch.

"I'm for Lennie!" some of them said, and others said, "I'm for Max!"

The wagons started off. But the hill was not steep. Neither wagon could pick up much speed. Max ran into a fence, and Lennie's wagon hit a rock and turned over.

Teeney got there just as the race ended. "That wasn't anything at all!" she said, and she went home.

In a little while Jo Ann went home, too. Teeney was at the back door. "Did anybody see Baby?" she asked.

"Did you have her out there?" asked Jo Ann.

"Yes, and I put her down when I went up the street," said Teeney. "Now I can't find her anywhere."

CHAPTER NINE

# Skipper

They looked all over the yard. They even looked in the house, although Teeney said, "I didn't take Baby in. I know I didn't."

"Maybe somebody hid her, for a joke," said Jo Ann. The girls went next door and asked Brenda if she had seen Baby.

"Is she gone?" asked Brenda.

"She was in the backyard, and now we can't find her," said Jo Ann.

Brenda's mother looked out the kitchen window. Jo Ann asked her, "Did you see anyone in our yard a while ago?"

"No, I didn't," said Brenda's mother.

"Teeney's doll is gone," said Jo Ann, "and I thought—"

"Did the doll have on a blue dress?" asked Brenda's mother.

"Yes!" said Teeney.

"I saw Skipper go past the window with something blue in his mouth," said Brenda's mother, "and I wondered what it was."

Brenda began to call, "Skipper, Skipper—here, Skip!"

The little dog came out from under the porch.

Brenda pointed her finger at him. "Did you take Teeney's doll?"

Skipper lay flat on the ground and put his paws over his nose.

Jo Ann was looking under the porch. "I see something—"

Teeney ducked her head and went under the porch. They heard her say, "Here she is." She came out with Baby in her arms.

She looked at the doll. She began to scream.

"Teeney!" said Jo Ann. Then she saw. The doll's face was gone.

Brenda's mother came running out. "What on earth—!"

"Teeney's doll—just look!" said Brenda.

"Oh!" said her mother. "Skipper licked the paint off."

"Will it make him sick?" asked Brenda.

Teeney was on her way home. Jo Ann followed her. Teeney was still screaming. Nyda met her at the door.

"Skipper licked the paint off her doll," said Jo Ann.

"She'll have to learn to take care of her things," said Nyda. "Stop that noise, Teeney. You shouldn't have left your doll out there."

"She knows it," said Jo Ann, "and you leave her alone!"

Teeney shut herself in the bedroom. She stopped crying. The house grew quiet.

Jo Ann sat on the back step.

Brenda came over. "Skipper is sorry," she said.

"That won't do any good," said Jo Ann.

Brenda sat down by her. "Teeney can't adopt Baby now, can she? I guess she can't ever get another doll from The Toy House."

"She didn't like it here till after she got her doll," said Jo Ann. "Now she's never going to like it here again."

"Your lunch is ready," said Nyda, and Jo Ann went in.

"I called your sister, but she won't come out," said Nyda.

Jo Ann went to the bedroom door. "Teeney?" she said.

There was no answer.

Jo Ann looked in the bedroom. She went out and told Nyda, "Teeney isn't in there."

"Look under the bed," said Nyda.

But Teeney wasn't under the bed. She was nowhere in the house.

"I don't know how she could have got out," said Nyda. "I never heard a sound."

Jo Ann took another look in the bedroom. Teeney's doll was gone, too.

"That child!" Nyda was saying. "Now I'll have to go looking for her."

"I'll find her," said Jo Ann.

# CHAPTER TEN

# The Party

Maggie was out in her yard. Jo Ann asked her if Teeney had gone by.

"Yes," said Maggie. "She was carrying something—I couldn't see what."

Jo Ann went on up the street. She was nearly to The Toy House when she met Teeney coming back. Teeney had cried until her eyes and nose were red.

Jo Ann took hold of her hand. "Come on. Let's go home."

They walked together.

"Where is Baby?" asked Jo Ann.

"I left her," said Teeney.

"At The Toy House?"

"Yes," said Teeney.

"What did Mrs. Lacey say?" asked Jo Ann.

"Nothing," said Teeney. "I didn't stay."

Nyda was cross when they got home. "I'm supposed to look after you, and how can I when you run away?"

"She won't do it any more," said Jo Ann.

Mamma came home. She had a surprise—some pieces of yarn in a package.

"I saw this in a store by the hotel," she said. "They're to wear in your hair. See? It's a thick kind of yarn, and every piece is a different color. I thought you ought to have *something* new for tomorrow. And I got something for myself." She held up a little blue scarf as thin as a spider web.

"It's pretty, Mamma," said Jo Ann.

"I'll wear it around my neck," said Mamma. "It's been a long time since I went to a party. I guess I haven't been to one since I was a girl."

Then she looked at their faces. "What's the matter?"

Jo Ann told her what had happened.

"Oh, my!" said Mamma, and she took Teeney on her lap and held her. "We'll see about getting you another doll."

"Not at The Toy House." Teeney was almost crying again. "They won't ever let me have anything any more."

"We'll see about it," said Mamma. "Anyway, Jo Ann can still adopt her doll, and we can all go to the party."

"I'm not going," said Teeney.

"Why, Teeney—," said Mamma.

Teeney slid off Mamma's lap. "I'm not *going!*"

Mamma looked worried. "I can't ask Lulu or Nyda to stay with you. They have other things to do on Sunday."

"I'll stay by myself," said Teeney.

"Oh, you can't do that." Mamma folded the blue scarf and put it away. "I'll start supper."

Afterward, when they were outside, Jo Ann told Teeney, "If you don't go tomorrow, Mamma will have to stay with you. And she wants to go."

Teeney only looked at her.

"I know you don't want to go," said Jo Ann, "but you *could,* couldn't you?"

"No," said Teeney.

The next day Mamma helped Jo Ann get ready. Anita was adopting a doll, too, and Jo Ann was going with her.

"Are you sure you can get to The Toy House by yourselves?" asked Mamma.

"Anita's mother is going with us," said Jo Ann. "I'd rather *you* were going, Mamma." She gave Teeney a look. "It's not right for you to stay home."

"You can tell me all about it," said Mamma.

"It's not right," Jo Ann said again, "when you

64

wanted to go and you got your scarf to wear." She gave Teeney another look.

Teeney said something. They could hardly hear her.

"What?" asked Mamma.

"I *might* go," said Teeney.

"Are you sure?" asked Mamma. "Are you sure you feel like it?"

"Yes," said Teeney.

"Then let's get ready as fast as we can," said Mamma.

They were only a little late to the party. When they went into the playroom, Mrs. Lacey was making a speech. The Doll Man met them at the door.

"I was afraid you weren't coming, I really was," he whispered. "Just sit down over there."

They sat in the back row of chairs. They saw five or six other girls with their mothers or older sisters. Each girl had a doll.

The room was decorated with crepe paper, and there were flowers, besides. Up in the corner there was a table with a cover over it. The cover was pulled up on one side, and underneath it they could see a bowl of punch and a big white cake.

"See the cake, Teeney?" asked Jo Ann.

But Teeney wouldn't look. She sat with her head down.

Mrs. Lacey finished her speech. "We are glad you could be here for our party. This is a day we have all been waiting for. Now as I call your names, will you please come forward?"

She began to read from a list of names. "Anita Lopez, Mary Ann Zimmer, Esther Ross—" One after another, the girls went to the front, and Mrs. Lacey gave them their adoption certificates. Each certificate was rolled up and tied with a ribbon.

She called Jo Ann's name. Jo Ann tried to look happy as she took her certificate, but she was thinking of Teeney, and she wasn't happy at all.

"Now," said Mrs. Lacey, "I hope you will have many good times with your dolls, and—"

The Doll Man went up and said something to her.

"Oh!" said Mrs. Lacey. "There is one more." And she called Teeney's name!

Teeney looked at Mamma.

"She called you," said Mamma.

"What for?" asked Teeney.

"I don't know," said Mamma. "Go and see."

Teeney got out of her chair. She walked slowly up to the front. Mrs. Lacey gave her a certificate.

"But I don't have any—," began Teeney.

She stopped. The Doll Man was holding out a doll to her.

Teeney said, "It's Baby!"

It was Baby, looking just as she had looked before. Her face was smooth and pink and white. She had her smile. She had her dimple.

Teeney took Baby and her certificate. She ran back to her seat and hid her face against Mamma.

Mamma said, "Sit up. There's someone here to talk to you."

It was The Doll Man. "I fixed Baby for you," he said. "A little paint, and she was as good as new."

"After what happened, she was afraid you wouldn't let her adopt a doll," said Mamma.

"She'd taken good care of Baby for a long time before the accident," said The Doll Man. "And when the accident happened, she did the right thing. She brought her to The Toy House. Yes, that really was the right thing. It was like taking Baby to the hospital."

Mrs. Lacey came by and told them to join the party. They all had punch and cake. Teeney and Jo Ann met the other girls who had adopted dolls. Mamma talked with some of the other mothers. It was a friendly party.

Mamma and Jo Ann and Teeney were the last to leave. They went out through the doll room. Mamma stopped before the china doll with the blue eyes and the shiny black hair.

"I see she's still here," she said.

"Yes," said Mrs. Lacey. "Such a nice doll, but

nobody wants to give her a home. I suppose it's because she's so old-fashioned."

Mamma started to speak. She stopped and started again. "I'd like—I mean, I wish— Maybe I could buy her from you."

"We don't sell anything at The Toy House," said Mrs. Lacey. "It's a rule."

"I know, but I thought—" Mamma looked at the doll. The doll seemed to look back at her.

Teeney said, "If Mamma had it, it would have a good home."

Mrs. Lacey asked Mamma, "You want a doll? You have your two girls, and still you want a doll?"

"I never had a doll," said Mamma.

Mrs. Lacey went to the shelf. She took down the china doll and put it in Mamma's hands.

They left The Toy House together—Jo Ann, Teeney, and Mamma. They went out through the iron gate and past the silver willow trees. The girls with their dolls looked up at Mamma with *her* doll.

Teeney said, "Mamma, you didn't get a certificate."

"She doesn't need one," said Jo Ann.

## About the Author

Clyde Robert Bulla is one of America's best known writers for young people today. The broad scope of his interests has led him to write more than fifty fine books on a variety of subjects, including travel, history, science, and music. He has been widely praised for his rare ability to write simply yet with great warmth and sensitivity. Mr. Bulla was given the Silver Medal of the Commonwealth of California for his distinguished contribution to the field of children's books, and in 1972 his book *Pocahontas and the Strangers* received the Christopher Award.

Clyde Bulla's early years were spent on a farm near King City, Missouri, and only after the chores were done could he devote himself to reading and writing. He now lives and works in the bustling city of Los Angeles. When he is not busy writing a book, he loves to travel.

## About the Artist

Wendy Watson now lives in the heart of New York City, but her illustrations usually reflect her happy memories of growing up in a large family in rural Vermont. She is the illustrator of *Father Fox's Pennyrhymes*, an A.L.A. Notable Children's Book for 1971, and a leading nominee for the 1971 National Book Award. A graduate of Bryn Mawr College, she has illustrated more than twenty books, some of which she has also written herself.